HOW
Go
Ca

by Gail Page

BLOOMSBURY
LIN NEW YORK SYDNEY

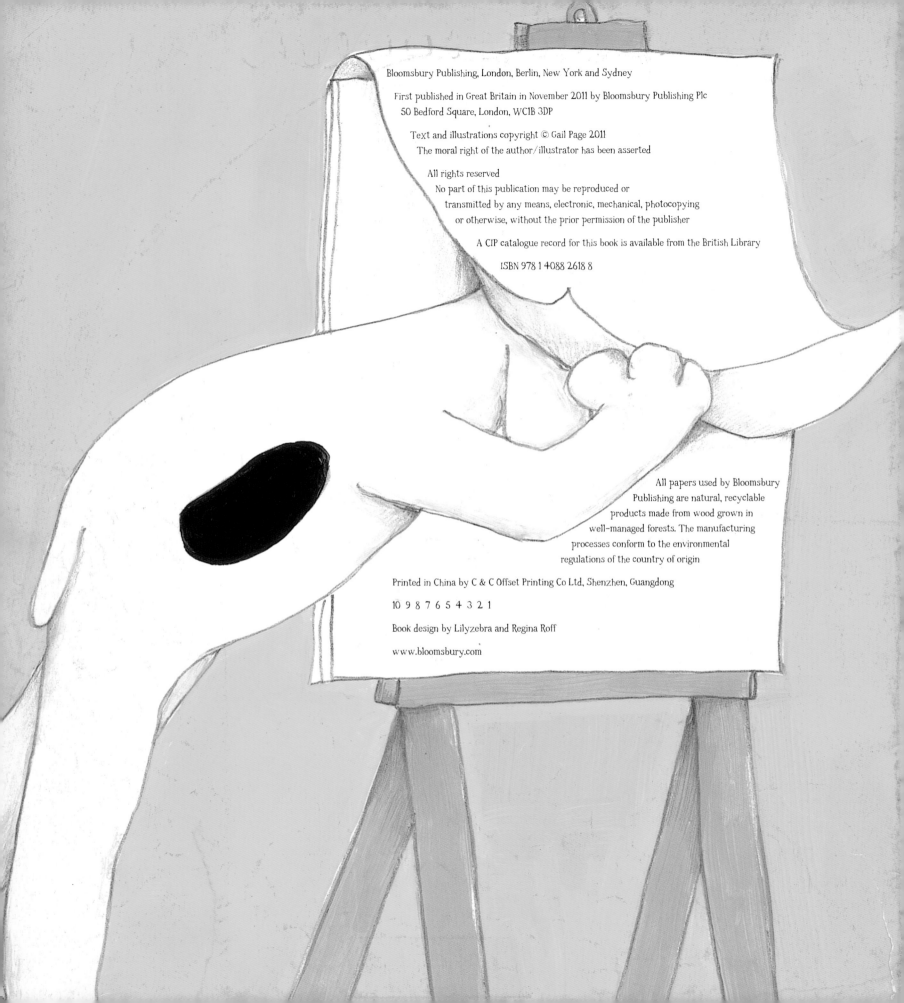

Bloomsbury Publishing, London, Berlin, New York and Sydney

First published in Great Britain in November 2011 by Bloomsbury Publishing Plc
50 Bedford Square, London, WC1B 3DP

Text and illustrations copyright © Gail Page 2011
The moral right of the author/illustrator has been asserted

A CIP catalogue record for this book is available from the British Library

ISBN 978 1 4088 2618 8

All papers used by Bloomsbury
Publishing are natural, recyclable
products made from wood grown in
well-managed forests. The manufacturing
processes conform to the environmental
regulations of the country of origin

Printed in China by C & C Offset Printing Co Ltd, Shenzhen, Guangdong

10 9 8 7 6 5 4 3 2 1

Book design by Lilyzebra and Regina Roff

www.bloomsbury.com

Dedicated to Robert Shetterly

Bobo was good.
He liked to help.

So when Mr. Hiccup asked Mrs. Birdhead
if someone could look after his kitten,

Bonkers wasn't just **very cute,**

he was also very . . .

NAU

Bobo tried all the tricks he knew.

Sit was **difficult.**

Fetch was **worse.**

Stay was a **complete disaster.**

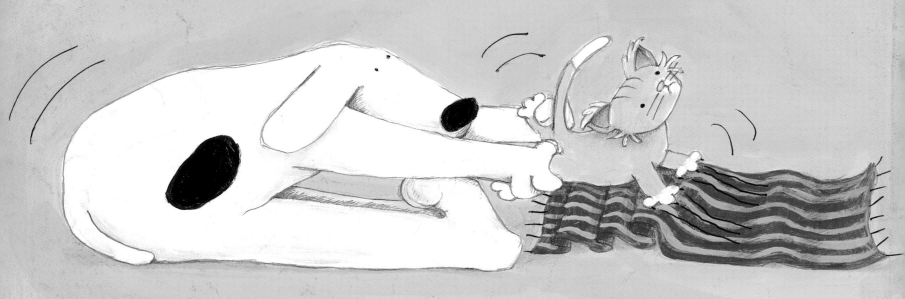

Nothing worked.

How could Bobo teach Bonkers to be a good cat?

Luckily, he knew **just** who to call.

Lesson #1:
Cats are **sneaky.**
You never see them coming.

Lesson #3:
Cats are stretchy.

It helps them balance and **pounce!**

Lesson #4:
Cats are very clean.

But they **don't** like water.

Lesson #5:
Cats like to climb.

And **they** always land on their feet.

In no time at all, the lessons were done.
Now Bobo knew all about cats.

Cats Sneak.

bark bark bark bark

Cats Chat.

meow meow meow

Cats Stretch.

Cats are
Clean.

Cats Climb.

But **Bobo** taught Bonkers something too . . .

How to take a **cat** nap.

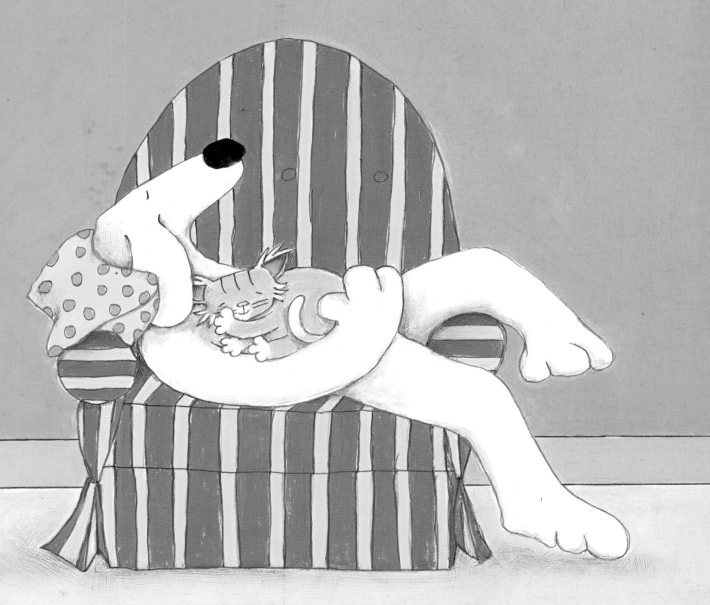

The end.